The
Annoying
Team

by Ilene Cooper
illustrated by Colin Paine

For Joshua Arjun Werth.
Thanks for the idea.
I.C.

To Angela
C.P.

Library of Congress Cataloging-in-Publication Data
Cooper, Ilene.
The Annoying Team / by Ilene Cooper ; illustrated by Colin Paine.
     p. cm. — (Road to reading. Mile 5)
Summary: Tim starts the Annoying Team to get back at the third-grade bully,
but things get out of hand as the group's activities expand.
ISBN 0-307-26512-9 (pbk.) — ISBN 0-307-46512-8 (GB)
[1. Behavior—Fiction. 2. Schools—Fiction. 3. Bullies—Fiction.] I. Paine,
Colin, ill. II. Title. III. Series.

PZ7.C7856 An 2002
[Fic]—dc21   2001023584

A GOLDEN BOOK • New York
Golden Books Publishing Company, Inc. New York, New York 10106

ISBN: 0-307-26512-9 (pbk)
ISBN: 0-307-46512-8 (GB)

10 9 8 7 6 5 4 3 2 1

Contents

1

Bugged!

Tim Adler put down his tray on the lunchroom table. His friend, Alex Parker, was already digging into the cafeteria special, chili. Tim didn't feel like eating.

He had always liked school. He got good grades. Teachers liked him. But now he was beginning to have stomachaches on school mornings. There was nothing worse than opening your eyes and thinking about your stomach.

Alex looked up from his chili. "Hey, Tim, what does *annoying* mean?"

"Huh?" said Tim.

"My sister told me I was annoying."

Tim looked at Alex. He was really enjoying his chili. Alex enjoyed all food. He was like a human garbage can.

"Annoying?" Tim repeated. "It's, like, when you bother somebody. When you bug them."

Alex smiled. There was chili on his front teeth. "Yeah, I was bugging her."

Somebody was bugging Tim, too. That's why he had a stomachache. When Tim started third grade, he made a very bad discovery. He was short. In kindergarten, first grade, and second grade, everyone had been the same size. A few kids were tall, but no one was really small. Now it seemed Tim was small. And Jon Ferguson was big. He was so big, he could be a fifth grader. He was a bully, too.

Jon had started calling him Toddler on

the first day of school. Then he came up with a new nickname—Tiny Tim.

"Hey, Tiny Tim."

Tim looked up. Standing next to the table were Jon and his friend Ron. Ron copied whatever Jon did.

"You and your pal having a good lunch?" Jon asked with a smirk.

"Sure they are," Ron answered for them. "Tim and Alex want to grow up big and strong."

"Tim's got a long way to go before he gets big," Jon said to Ron. "But Alex is getting big—and fat!" Before Tim could say anything, they walked away, laughing.

Alex pushed his chili bowl away with a sigh. "My mom says I should ignore Jon."

"Moms always say stuff like that," Tim scowled. "I don't think we should ignore them. I think we should get back at them. Make them stop bothering us."

Alex looked nervous. "They're bigger than we are."

"But we're smarter."

"We are?"

Well, I am, Tim thought. But he didn't say that out loud. "I think we're smart enough to take them."

Alex looked at Tim doubtfully.

Tim had an idea. "Look, we can be a team. We can *annoy* them. We'll call ourselves the Annoying Team."

"The Annoying Team?" Alex frowned.

Tim was getting excited. "Yes. Instead of letting them bug us, we'll bug them. And pretty soon they'll leave us alone."

Alex took a big swig of his milk. Now he had a milk mustache. "What will we do?"

Tim's excitement faded fast. What could they do? Alex was looking at him. Waiting.

Then Tim had an idea. "What does Miss Gomez hate more than anything?"

Alex thought for a second. "When we're not prepared to work."

"Exactly."

Miss Gomez always got mad whenever kids forgot their homework. Or if they didn't know the words to a song they had to sing for assembly. Her mouth would bunch up like she had just eaten a sour cherry. She'd shake her head and say, "You must always be prepared to work."

Tim tipped back his chair and smiled. "We're going to make sure that, tomorrow morning, Jon Ferguson is not prepared to work."

2
Bugging Back

"We're not supposed to be in here," Alex said nervously.

Tim looked around the empty classroom. "There's no rule that says we can't come in early to study."

"But we're not here to study," Alex pointed out.

"We'll study after we take Jon's pencils," Tim said.

Now that it was time to put his plan into action, Tim felt uncomfortable. He didn't want Alex to know that, though.

Giving Alex a small push, Tim followed him over to Jon's messy desk. If there was one thing Jon was proud of, it was his pencils. Each one had his name on it, stamped in gold. Tim grabbed two pencils off Jon's desk. Then he lifted the desk lid, reached in, and took out the last one.

Alex watched Tim stuff the pencils into his sweatshirt pocket. "This is stealing," he said.

"No, it isn't. We're going to give the pencils back."

"We are?" Alex asked with surprise.

"Sure. We have to let Jon know who is driving him crazy."

"Oh." Alex looked as unhappy at this news as he was about taking the pencils.

"We're just not going to give them back right away."

"When—" Before Alex could finish his question, the first bell rang. Tim and Alex slipped into their seats. The rest of the class filed in.

Jon walked by Tim and said, "Hey, Tiny Tim. Want a pinch to grow an inch?" Then he ruffled Tim's hair.

Tim hated anyone touching his hair, even his parents, and they had a right to. Jerking his head away, Tim said, "Quit it!"

Jon just laughed at him and went to his seat. Tim was glad that the Annoying Team was on the move.

First period was math. Tim knew they were having a quiz this morning. That was one of the reasons he had decided nabbing pencils might be a good place to start.

Tim's eyes were trained on Jon. A few minutes after nine, Jon noticed his pencils weren't on his desk. He frowned and

looked on the floor to see if he had dropped them.

Miss Gomez passed out the quizzes. For a moment, Tim forgot to watch Jon. The math questions were hard. When he glanced back, Jon was looking inside his desk.

"All right, class," Miss Gomez said. "You have twenty minutes. Begin the quiz."

"Miss Gomez," Jon waved his hand, "my pencils are gone."

Miss Gomez frowned. "You know a student must always be prepared to work."

"They were here yesterday...."

Miss Gomez's frown deepened. "You are holding up the whole class. Alex, lend him a pencil."

Alex leaned across the aisle and gave a

pencil to Jon. Jon scowled at him. Tim couldn't help but smile at how well his plan was working.

If that wasn't enough, Miss Gomez had the students trade and grade each other's papers. Tim got a 100. Alex graded Jon's paper, then handed it back. He gave Tim the thumbs-down sign.

Later at recess, Tim heard Jon say he hadn't done well on the test because his lucky pencils were missing.

Tim punched Alex. "They were his lucky pencils!"

Alex rubbed his arm. "I heard. I heard. That will make him even madder when he finds out we took them."

Tim just laughed. He was beginning to enjoy this. "What should we take from him next?"

"Weren't the pencils enough?"

"Alex, we're supposed to be a team here. Every time I come up with an idea, you want to figure out a way not to do it."

Alex sighed.

"How about his social studies book?" Tim asked. "We usually read out loud from those in the afternoon."

Getting the social studies book was even easier than the pencils. Before social studies came science. All the kids worked in different parts of Room 301 on their experiments. Tim waited until Jon seemed involved with his bird feeder and then he took the social studies book off Jon's desk. He put it in the cloakroom.

When it was time for social studies, Jon looked frantically for his book while Betsy Bauer read aloud.

"Excuse me, Betsy," Miss Gomez said, interrupting her. "Jon, what is the problem?"

"My book is gone. It was right here on my desk."

"Jon, you mean to tell me you are not prepared to work for the second time in one day?" Miss Gomez was angry.

"Something's going on—" Jon tried to explain, but Miss Gomez stopped him.

"This is unacceptable. You will sit quietly and listen while your classmates are reading. Then, for homework, you will write a report about what you heard."

"But, Miss Gomez!" Jon howled.

"Betsy, continue reading."

Tim leaned back in his chair. Better and better. This annoying stuff was fun.

3
Victory

The next morning, Tim said to Alex, "It's time for stage two."

"What's stage two?" Alex asked.

"We let Jon know we took his stuff."

"Uh-oh," was all Alex said.

Tim knew stage two had to be handled very carefully. Maybe it would help to have other people on their side. That shouldn't be too hard. After all, Jon bullied lots of kids.

It was a sunny day, warm for fall. Tim and Alex sat down on a stone bench outside the school. Tim looked around the schoolyard. Penny Franklin was heading toward the front door. Penny would be perfect for his plan. He called her over. She was a big girl, almost as big as Jon.

"Hey," she said, looking down at Tim.

"You don't like Jon, do you?" he asked.

"No, I don't. He ruined my summer. He made fun of me because I don't like to swim. He kept pretending to push me in the pool." Penny looked at Tim suspiciously. "What's it to you?"

"He's been making fun of us, too," Tim began. He told Penny about the Annoying Team and what they had been up to.

Penny clapped her hands. "I want to be on the Annoying Team."

Tim hadn't pictured Penny as an actual team member. But she seemed more into it than Alex. He saw the advantages of Penny joining up.

"What can I do?" Penny asked.

"You can help us with the next part of the plan," Tim said. "We're going to start telling people we took Jon's stuff."

"I'll spread the word to my friends. They won't tell Jon."

"Okay. We'll tell a couple of the guys."

By lunchtime, the news about the Annoying Team was getting around. As Tim waited in line to get into the cafeteria, several kids came up to him.

"That Jon is a bully," one kid said.

"What are you going to do to him next?" a girl asked.

Tim made a decision. "Come to Jon's table after you finish lunch," he said. "You'll see then."

Tim was nervous as he ate his cheese sandwich. Alex was nervous, too. "Do you think this will work?" he asked.

" 'Course it will," Tim said. He tried to sound more sure than he felt.

At the end of lunch, Tim, Alex, and Penny got together. The kids from Room 301 saw them heading toward Jon's table, and most of them came over, too. Jon was slurping his soup when Tim and the others walked up. Ron saw them first. He gave Jon a nudge.

"What do you want, Toddler?" Jon growled.

Tim's hand shook as he pulled Jon's pencils out of his pocket.

"You took them!" Jon said, half rising from his seat.

Tim moved back. "Yeah. We took your social studies book, too."

"Who's 'we'?" Jon demanded.

Tim pointed back at Alex and Penny. With a wave, he included the other kids standing behind him, even if they weren't exactly team members. "The Annoying Team." He tried to make the words sound bold, but they came out in a squeak.

"The Annoying Team? What's that?" Ron asked.

"You bug us, we bug you right back," Tim said.

"You took my stuff just because I called you names?" Jon looked surprised.

"That's right," Tim said. "And we're going to keep annoying you unless you stop."

"Aw, you can't make me," Jon said. But he didn't look so sure.

"Here's the deal," Tim said boldly. "We'll give you back your stuff. If you leave us alone, we'll leave you alone. But if you start ragging us, well, we're really going to go after you."

Jon looked at the kids clustered around the table. There were a lot of them. "I was only kidding around," he muttered.

"Then we have a deal?" Tim asked.

Jon shrugged. "When do I get my stuff back?"

"As soon as we get to the room."

"I could tell Miss Gomez on you," Jon said. Tim just looked at him. He knew Jon would never tattle to a teacher. "But I won't," Jon said, defeated.

Tim walked away, feeling like a winner. The kids that followed him asked if they could be on the Annoying Team.

"Sure," Tim said grandly. "Why not?"

4

Another Annoying Idea

Tim was so proud of himself, his mouth hurt from smiling. When Miss Gomez left the room for a moment, he got up and gave Jon back his book and his pencils. All the kids were watching.

Jon didn't say anything. He just shoved the stuff in his desk.

Tim smiled some more. He swaggered back to his desk. After school, kids clapped him on the back. They told him it had been great watching Jon finally get what he deserved.

That night, Tim told his sister Annie all about it.

Tim and Annie were twins, but they were in different classrooms. They were both small, although that didn't seem to be a problem for a girl. But Tim's brown hair was curly while Annie's lighter hair hung straight.

They didn't look at all like their eleven-year-old sister, Melissa. Melissa had dark, curly hair.

"It was so cool," Tim told Annie. "Jon just sat there."

"And you don't think he'll give you any more trouble?" Annie asked.

"Nah. Now there's a whole bunch of us on the Annoying Team. What can he do against most of the class?"

"So you're going to keep up this Annoying Team?" Annie asked.

"Sure," Tim answered. "Why not?"

"You'll have to come up with more annoying things to do," Annie pointed out. Tim looked at Annie with surprise. He hadn't thought of that.

But it didn't take him long to start thinking that way. He couldn't help it. Kids kept coming up and pestering him at school the next day.

"So what's the next move for the Annoying Team?" Judd Kessler wanted to know.

"We have to come up with another annoying thing," Penny told Tim. "Everybody wants to be annoying."

Even Alex was excited now that the Annoying Team was a success. "Tim, I was thinking. Maybe we could go down to the 7-Eleven and say we want to buy Big Gulps and then change our minds."

Tim just looked at Alex. "Why?"

"Well," Alex said uncertainly, "that would annoy the clerks."

"But we don't have any reason to annoy them," Tim tried to explain.

"Oh," was all Alex said. He looked disappointed.

That's the problem, Tim thought as he lay in bed that night, trying to sleep. *We don't really have a reason to annoy anyone else.* Of course, they could just pick on someone for no reason, but that didn't seem right.

Tim tried to come up with a plan the next day, too. Then, as Room 301 was packing up for the day, Miss Gomez said something that instantly sparked his brain.

"Children, I won't be in school tomorrow. You will have a substitute. Mr. Potter will be back. You remember Mr. Potter."

"Yes!" Tim whispered to himself.

Mr. Potter was like a gift fallen out of the sky. He was the worst sub they had ever had. He had canceled recess because two girls were talking. And he had made them so late for a special assembly that Room 301 had missed it.

Tim pushed away the paper with his math homework on it and tore a fresh piece of paper out of his notebook. In big block letters, he wrote the words **MR. POTTER**. Then he began listing the many ways Mr. Potter could be bugged.

5

The Sub

The next morning, some of the kids from Room 301 were waiting for Tim in the schoolyard. That was okay. He was ready for them. He called a meeting of the Annoying Team.

"The Annoying Team has somebody new to annoy," Tim began. "Our sub, Mr. Potter."

"Oh, good one," Penny said.

"Yeah, he yelled at me last time he was here," Alex said.

"Half the time he was mean to us. The other half he looked scared of us," Judd remembered. "He deserves to be annoyed."

"Exactly," Tim agreed. "So here's what we're going to do...."

When the first bell rang, the Annoying Team, which was now most of the class, marched into Room 301. They were smiling and giggling. While Penny stood guard, Tim took the lesson plan that Miss Gomez had left for Mr. Potter. He hid it under her desk.

By the time Mr. Potter came into the room, all of the kids were sitting quietly in their seats.

"Uh, good morning, class," Mr. Potter said, clearing his throat. With his orange shirt and orangish-red hair, Mr. Potter looked like a tall carrot. He checked the desk. "I don't see a lesson plan," he said.

"We can tell you what we do," Tim said helpfully.

"Uh, thank you"—Mr. Potter looked at the seating chart—"uh, Tim. I guess you'll have to."

"We're studying birds in science," Tim said. That part was the truth, anyway.

"Oh, that's interesting," Mr. Potter replied.

"Today we're doing birdcalls."

"Birdcalls!"

"Yes, we broke into groups and studied one kind of bird and its call. Now we're going to give the calls in class," Penny informed Mr. Potter.

Tim looked at Penny with admiration. His heart had been beating like a boat motor when he'd mentioned birdcalls. Penny acted like giving birdcalls was no more unusual than reciting the multiplication tables.

Mr. Potter stared at the class as if he wasn't sure whether to believe them. Finally, he just shrugged and said, "Okay. Who's supposed to start?"

That was Judd's cue. "We're the robins," he said. Then Judd and two other kids got up in front of the class and made whistling noises. They didn't sound like robins. They barely sounded like birds, but the class clapped noisily for them.

Mr. Potter looked even more uncomfortable. "Am I supposed to give you grades?"

Tim answered quickly. He didn't want notes left behind for Miss Gomez like, "Robins: B−."

"Oh, no," Tim said, "we're just supposed to share the calls with the class."

"Okay," Mr. Potter said. "I wouldn't

know how to grade this, anyway. Who's next?"

The woodpeckers were up next. Tim had asked Jon and Ron if they wanted to be woodpeckers. It seemed better if they were part of the Annoying Team, too. Otherwise they might turn on Tim.

Jon had thought about it and said, "Yeah, I don't mind being on the team."

Jon and Ron made excellent woodpeckers. They mixed in their whistling noises with head butting. That was supposed to be pecking.

The class loved it, cheering them on.

Mr. Potter stopped them. "This is getting out of hand, boys."

"Aw, we were just having fun with it," Ron complained.

"Next group," Mr. Potter said.

Tim got up with Alex and Penny. "We're, uh, the parakeets." It was hard not to laugh.

"Parakeets! They're not birds found in the wild," Mr. Potter grumbled.

"Not birds found in the wild," Penny repeated in a parakeet-ish voice.

"Are you mocking me, young lady?" Mr. Potter asked.

"Parakeets aren't wild birds," Tim said quickly. "But Miss Gomez thought they'd be interesting because they talk and all."

"This is very strange," Mr. Potter said. He ran a hand through his carrot-colored hair.

"Very strange, very strange," Alex mimicked.

"You know, I think you'd better save the birdcalls until your teacher gets back."

"Teacher gets back," Penny repeated. The rest of the kids laughed out loud.

"Sit down!" Mr. Potter said.

The parakeets went quietly to their seats.

That was the way the day went. Tim had told the kids to be good for the next class, which was math. But during English, they kept asking to go to the bathroom. Mr. Potter looked suspicious after the second request. He tried to tell one of the girls to wait, but when she looked like she might cry, he gave her a bathroom pass. He told Jon he definitely couldn't go, but Jon argued that Mr. Potter was being unfair to boys.

The Annoying Team congratulated themselves during lunch. Tim declared the afternoon devoted to art. Room 301 had art class once a week, but on Friday and only for a half hour.

The kids told Mr. Potter they were painting pictures of their teacher for the school art show. "Shouldn't you wait for Miss Gomez?" Mr. Potter asked.

"They're due tomorrow," Penny said primly. "And you're the only teacher we've got right now."

So Mr. Potter posed for most of the afternoon.

The pictures were too funny. Most of them showed Mr. Potter as some sort of carrot-person. As he walked around the room, he seemed a little hurt.

The class was putting away the art supplies when Tim whispered to Penny, "Do you think we went too far?" He kept seeing that sad look on Mr. Potter's face.

"Heck no. He's not even going to leave a note for Miss Gomez saying we were bad. If he did that, we would know we went too far."

Tim decided that Penny was right. They had been thoroughly annoying, and there wasn't any price to pay. Yes, the Annoying Team was a real success.

6
The Piano Recital

Now Tim had a new nickname—Captain. He was captain of the Annoying Team. Tim liked it much better than Tiny Tim.

For exactly one day, the kids in Room 301 were happy to enjoy how annoying they had been. But after that, they started bugging Tim again. What annoying thing were they going to do next?

The pressure to come up with an idea closed around him. If that wasn't bad enough, he came home from school to find he had to spend Saturday afternoon at his sister Melissa's piano recital.

The next day, Melissa stood blocking the door to Tim's bedroom. "You can't wear that!"

Tim looked down at his clothes. "Why not?"

"You need to wear a white shirt. And maybe a tie."

"A tie! I don't have a tie, except that stupid bow tie I wore for my first-grade picture."

Melissa got a stubborn look on her face. She could be very stubborn.

Tim pushed past her. "Mom," he yelled down the stairs, "I don't have to wear a tie, do I?"

His mother stood at the foot of the stairs. "It might be nice...." She took another look at Tim's face. "But I guess you don't have to. Why don't you just change into a regular shirt instead of a sweatshirt."

Melissa smirked as he went back to his room to change shirts. Tim stuck his tongue out at her.

As the day wore on, things in the Adler house became hectic. Mr. Adler was trying to get the kids to eat the sandwiches he'd made. Mrs. Adler was fixing a droopy hem on Melissa's dress. Melissa kept combing her hair and whining that her curls didn't look right.

"At least she has curls," Annie sighed.

Finally, they were ready to go. In the car, Melissa chattered on about the recital. "I'm going to play last," Melissa said.

"You already told us that," Tim said. "About ten times," he added under his breath.

"That's because Mrs. Rose is saving the best for last," Melissa continued.

Tim and Annie rolled their eyes. *Melissa is annoying without even trying,* Tim thought.

The Adler family walked into Mrs. Rose's living room. A big piano stood in front of the window. The regular furniture had been moved against the walls to make room for chairs for the audience.

"Hello, Adlers!" Mrs. Rose came over to greet them. "Melissa, are you ready to play?"

"Yes, Mrs. Rose," Melissa answered. But for the first time, Tim thought she looked a little nervous.

The family took their seats. After a few seconds, Tim got up to go to the bathroom.

On his way back, Tim passed the bedroom of Mrs. Rose's son. Something caught his eye. On the dresser stood a big wire cage. Inside the cage were three small mice.

Boy, that kid is lucky, Tim thought. He had always wanted mice or guinea pigs. But his mother would wrinkle her nose, shake her head, and say, "No rodents."

Tim walked over to the cage. He opened the door and took out one of the mice. The thing he liked about mice was that they were so small. You could carry them in your pocket. He must seem like a giant to a mouse.

After a minute, Tim put the mouse back and returned to his seat. The room was filling up. It was almost time for the recital to begin.

Mrs. Rose stood in front of the piano and said, "Welcome, everyone. We have five wonderful students who want to share their music with you. First is Amy Kwan. She will play 'London Bridge Is Falling Down.' "

Amy was about five years old. She had to be helped onto the piano bench. But she played her song quickly and without any mistakes. *One down, four to go,* thought Tim.

Two more students played. Tim had to admit neither one was as good as Melissa. Then a girl about Melissa's age started to play "Home on the Range." Before she got halfway through, one of the mothers let out a shriek. A kid in the audience yelled, "Something's under my foot!"

"It's a mouse!" the piano player said.

She took her feet off the piano pedals and sat cross-legged on the bench.

Everything went crazy after that. Three mice were running around the living room. They were probably more scared than the people, but some of the grown-ups in the audience were pretty alarmed, too.

"Oh, dear," Mrs. Rose moaned. "How did this happen?"

Tim had a pretty good idea. He remembered opening the cage door, but he didn't remember closing it. "I'll get them," he volunteered. It seemed the least he could do.

It took a while. One of the parents found a mouse hiding behind the curtain, and Tim caught it. A white mouse kept darting across the living room before Tim

grabbed it in one hand. The piano player caught the last mouse as it tried to hide between the piano pedals. Mrs. Rose brought the cage into the living room, and one by one, the mice were put back into their wire home.

"Mice!" Melissa muttered. "When I need to be calm before I play."

Boy, Tim thought, *I really couldn't have annoyed Melissa any more if I'd wanted to.*

After all the excitement, things settled down slowly. There was lots of talking, but finally people put their chairs back in place. They listened to "Home on the Range," and then to Melissa's piece, "When the Saints Go Marching In." Everyone clapped along. It seemed like the right song after so much crashing and shouting.

Mrs. Rose had laid out a table of refreshments. As Tim was moving through the line to get some chocolate cake, he had an idea. A really bright idea. An Annoying Team idea.

"Are you okay?" Annie asked.

"Huh? Oh, sure." Tim dug into his cake. He could hardly wait until Monday.

7

A New Captain

The word went around the class on Monday that Tim wanted to see the Annoying Team after lunch. The buzz was so loud, Miss Gomez slapped her hand against the desk and called for quiet.

At lunch, the kids chowed down as fast as they could and moved into the school-yard.

"The next Annoying Team project," Tim announced, "is a contest."

There were *oohs* and *aahs*.

"How many of you have a brother or sister who really bugs you?"

Almost everyone raised a hand.

"Good. If you don't have a brother or sister, maybe you can pick a cousin or something," Tim went on.

"What about a baby-sitter?" Alex asked.

"Fine, a baby-sitter. Anybody who annoys you." Tim glared at Alex. "The thing is, I want you to annoy that person. Whoever does the best annoying gets a prize."

"What's the prize?" Penny wanted to know.

"To be captain of the Annoying Team for three days."

"Cool," said Judd.

Tim thought it was cool, too. He would be able to pass his job to somebody else for a couple of days. Let that person worry about coming up with annoying ideas. The new captain would see that being annoying wasn't as easy as it looked.

"Boy, all I have to do is look at my little sister's blankey, and she gets mad," Penny said.

"There you go," Tim nodded. "No one is easier to bug than someone you know really well. So let's meet here tomorrow morning. Then we'll pick a winner."

The next morning, all the kids on the Annoying Team came to school early. They couldn't wait to find out who had pulled off the most annoying prank. Everybody wanted to talk first.

"Okay, okay." Tim held up his hand. "One at a time."

Most of the annoying things the team members had done were pretty good. One girl had kept whistling a song her brother hated. Judd had made kissing noises on an extension phone while his older sister talked to her boyfriend.

Then Jon pushed his way to the middle of the circle. "I won."

"Oh yeah?" Tim challenged him. Even though Jon was now one of them, Tim still didn't like him.

"See, my sister is always calling me these weird nicknames—"

"Like what?" Tim interrupted.

Jon glared at him. "Never mind. Well, my sister has a pretty bad nickname herself. Ever since she was a baby, my parents have called her Chubbles."

"Chubbles?" Penny tried not to smile.

"Yeah, she hates it. So last night the prom committee met at our house. I made sure this picture of her was on the mantel. My mother made a fancy frame for it that says, 'Our Chubbles.' All of her friends saw it," Jon said with satisfaction. "They started calling her Chubbles, and now she says she wants to quit school."

Even Tim had to admit this was pretty impressive. Jon had practically ruined his sister's life.

Jon looked around. "So, I won, didn't I?" Most of the group nodded. "That means I get to be captain of the Annoying Team for the next three days."

"You sure do," Ron said loyally.

"So who are you going to annoy?" Tim asked.

"That's for me to know, and you to find out," Jon said.

"You know, you can't bug any of the team members," Tim said, trying not to sound nervous.

"That wasn't part of the deal," Jon replied. "But it doesn't matter. This will be bigger than anything we've done before." With that, he walked away.

Tim was not happy. He wanted someone to take over as the captain of the Annoying Team for a while, but he didn't want it to be Jon. And he didn't want Jon coming up with better ideas than he had.

This wasn't working out the way Tim thought it would.

Jon's first Annoying Team idea took place as Room 301 waited in the lunch line. Jon started a whispered message that went from one kid to the next: "Every few seconds drop your money."

Soon coins were clinking to the floor, and kids stooped to pick them up. The Annoying Team held up the whole lunch

line. Finally, the cafeteria manager, Mrs. Otis, had to come out from behind the counter to see what was going on. "Is this some silly joke?" she asked.

A couple of kids who were gathering their coins looked up guiltily. "No," they chorused.

By now, the line was backed up into the hallway. The students from other rooms were shoving, giggling, and making noise. It was all Mrs. Otis could do to get the line moving again.

Jon was laughing harder than anyone. Mrs. Otis stood over him, looking as though she'd like to dump a bowl of today's special—beanies and wienies— right on his head.

Even a gloomy Tim had to admit this was a very annoying prank. When Room

301 had acted up while Miss Gomez was gone, they had only bothered Mr. Potter. This coin dropping had thrown the whole lunch line into confusion.

The kids were laughing about it all afternoon. They seemed just as happy to have Jon for a captain as they had been with Tim. And Jon didn't worry about annoying people who didn't deserve it.

The next day was Jon's second day as captain of the Annoying Team. His plan was to mix all their leftover lunches—the gooey, gushy ones—drop the mess on the floor, and leave it there for the janitor to mop up.

"Why would we do a stupid thing like that?" Tim asked.

"Because he'll think it's throw-up," Jon answered with a frown.

"It would be a big mess," Ron said, laughing. "Huge."

A couple of the other kids agreed.

"But Mr. Harmon never did anything to us," Tim argued. "He's always nice to everybody."

"It's not about him," Jon said. "It's about mopping up barf. Besides, I'm the captain. I can order the team to do anything I want."

After school, Tim kicked a can all the way home. "The Annoying Team is supposed to bug people who are bugging us," he complained to Alex. "Not Mr. Harmon. Not even Mrs. Otis."

Alex nodded. "I didn't like seeing Mr. Harmon mop up that mess. Some of the kids thought it was funny, though."

"Well," Tim said with a sigh, "Jon is

only captain of the Annoying Team for one more day. He can't cause too much trouble."

"I don't know," Alex replied. "He said that tomorrow the Annoying Team is going to pull off its worst trick yet."

Worst? Trick? That didn't sound good. It didn't sound good at all.

8

The Worst Trick

When Tim got home, Annie was sitting at the kitchen table, worrying. "What's wrong, Annie?" Tim asked.

"The play."

Tim felt bad. He had been so caught up in the Annoying Team that he hadn't been paying much attention to Annie's life. Her play was part of a special school program tomorrow night. Annie had an important part.

"Do you have stage fright?" Tim asked.

Annie twirled a strand of hair. "I guess. There are so many things that can go wrong."

Tim pulled up a chair and sat across from her. "Like what?"

"Well, I know my lines, but I could forget them. Anybody could. And we all have to remember our moves. Then there are the toys."

"Toys?"

"The play is a mystery about toys. So we have to make sure they disappear and reappear at the right time."

"I see what you mean."

Annie nodded. "And what about the audience? What if they don't like the play?"

Tim made a face. "Oh, they'll like it. The parents will like it. They like anything their kids are in."

"But the whole school will be there," Annie moaned. "I don't care about the parents. I care about what the other kids think."

"You'll be great," Tim said stoutly. "Really, you will."

"I hope so." But Annie still looked worried.

The next day, it was Tim's turn to be worried. By the time he got to school, the Annoying Team was buzzing over Jon's latest idea.

"What did Jon come up with?" Tim asked Alex.

Alex didn't look happy. "We're going to ruin Room 302's play tonight."

"What!" Tim yelled.

"Some of the team members are going to take all the toys they need for their play," Alex told Tim.

"It's Annie's play! We can't do that."

"Well, that's the plan," Alex said.

Tim felt pains in his stomach. This was terrible.

Jon was explaining how he was going to pull off his plan. "See, they're going to put all the toys they need backstage this afternoon."

"How do you know?" Penny asked.

"I heard the kids who are in charge of the props talking about it."

"What are 'props'?" Penny interrupted.

"It's the stuff they use in plays," Jon said, glaring at her. "In this play, it's a bunch of toys."

"Why do they call them props?" Alex asked.

"I don't know," Jon said, practically yelling. "But I'll tell you what's going to happen to them. Tonight, before the play starts, some of us will sneak back there and take as many toys as we can."

"What if they catch us?" one of the girls asked.

Jon waved her question away. "They won't if we're careful."

"But they'll see us with the toys," Alex said.

"Nah, we'll just stuff them somewhere backstage."

Tim crossed his arms and spoke up. "Why did you think of this idea?"

Jon shrugged. "I don't like one of the kids in 302. The one who's in charge of the props. And then I started thinking, why should they put on the play, anyway? Why wasn't it our room?"

Some of the kids nodded. One of the girls said she'd been mad when she'd

found out 302 was doing a play in the special assembly.

"It should have been us," a boy named Will said.

Tim felt trapped. He had to say something that would make Jon change his plan. But most of the Annoying Team seemed excited about Jon's trick. Finally he said, "I don't think we should ruin their play."

Jon turned and looked at him. "Why not?"

"Well, it's not very nice."

Jon gave a mean laugh. "No, it's annoying. That's what the Annoying Team is all about, Tim. You invented it, remember?"

Now Tim's stomach really did hurt.

9

Burnt Toast

It was a good thing Miss Gomez didn't call on Tim that morning. He wasn't paying attention to anything she said. All he could think about was Annie's play. During math, he wrote down things he could do to make sure the play wasn't ruined.

1. Tell Jon Not to Take the Props.

That idea looked puny. Why would Jon listen to him? Jon was the captain of the Annoying Team. He had the right to do any annoying thing he wanted.

And whose fault was that? It had been his own idea to hand the job of captain over to somebody else.

2. Tell Annie.

Should I tell her? Tim wondered. Then Annie would have the stomachache. She could tell her teacher, but that would get Tim's room in trouble. It didn't seem fair to make Annie deal with all this. The Annoying Team was his problem.

3. Make the Annoying Team See That Ruining the Play Is a Very Bad Idea.

Tim stared at number three. It seemed as if almost everyone thought Jon's idea was pretty good. Oh, a few of the kids were a little scared, but nobody had said they didn't want to do it.

All morning, Tim worried. He worried until he didn't think he could worry anymore.

"Tim?"

Tim looked up. Miss Gomez was standing over him. What had he missed?

"I asked you to be class monitor while I go to the principal's office."

"Oh, okay," Tim said.

Tim walked to the front of the class. As soon as their teacher shut the door, some of the kids started talking to each other.

Tim stood in front of Miss Gomez's desk, the way the class monitor was supposed to, and watched the class. Nearly every person in 301 was on the Annoying Team. If he wanted to say something, this was the perfect time. But did he?

Suddenly, Tim knew he didn't have a choice. He felt scared. He felt weird. But he had to make the Annoying Team change their minds about messing up Room 302's play. If he didn't try, he'd feel even worse.

Tim cleared his throat. No one paid a bit of attention.

"Uh, hey!" He said it a little louder than he meant to. Everybody looked up now.

"What do you want, Adler?" Jon asked. He looked as if he knew something was going on.

Getting the words out was like spitting stones. But Tim finally said, "It's about tonight. The play."

"Yeah? What about it?" Jon asked.

"I don't think we should do it." There, he'd said it.

"Are you kidding? It's a great idea," Ron said.

"It's mean," Tim replied.

Jon said, "Aw, you just think it's mean because your sister is in that room."

"Yeah, she is, but it would be mean, anyway."

Jon left his seat and walked toward Tim. To Tim, Jon seemed taller than ever. "Did you forget? I'm the captain."

Tim didn't like the way Jon's fists were curling at his sides. Jon wouldn't hit him. Would he?

Tim faced the class again. He hoped they couldn't tell how scared he was. "Look," he said, "I started the Annoying Team because, well, because somebody was bugging me. But 302 hasn't done anything to us."

For a few seconds there was silence. Then Penny said, "It wasn't their fault the principal asked them to put on a play instead of us."

Good old Penny, Tim thought.

Then he said, "That's right. Anyway, what if we were putting on the play, and Annie's room was going to do something like this to us? How would we feel?"

Before anyone could say anything, Miss Gomez came back into the room. She looked around the room like a dog sniffing out trouble. "Is something going on? Jon, why are you away from your desk?" she asked.

Jon gestured toward the trash can. "Throwing something out," he muttered.

Both boys went back to their seats without another word. Miss Gomez told the class to take out their books for silent reading.

Maybe the other kids were reading silently, but Tim was trying to figure out if what he said had made one bit of difference. He looked at Jon. Jon didn't seem to be reading, either.

It had started raining. It rained so hard that recess was canceled. The students had to stay in during lunch, too.

Tim sat across from Alex and watched him eat the cafeteria special, Tuna-Noodle Surprise. The surprise was that it had a few potato chips sprinkled across the top.

Tim felt too upset to eat his cheese sandwich. None of his classmates had said anything to him. Most hadn't even looked his way. Even Alex was quiet. He just sat there, shoveling in the Tuna-Noodle Surprise.

Finally, Tim had to say, "So what do you think, Alex?"

"About what?"

"The play," Tim said impatiently.

Alex shrugged. "I'm not going to steal anything. It's dumb." He put down his fork. "Tim, I don't like the Annoying Team."

"I know," Tim replied glumly. "It got out of hand."

"I didn't like it before that. I didn't like it when you first thought it up."

Tim nodded. Maybe Alex had been the smart one all along.

Penny marched up to Tim. "I'm not doing the toy thing," she announced.

"You aren't?"

"Nope. And I'm quitting the Annoying Team," Penny added. "Most of the girls are quitting, too. We talked it over. Even if you're captain again, we don't want to do it anymore. Pretty soon kids are going to start annoying us. Then it will just be an annoying war."

Judd and a couple of the boys came over to the table. Judd said, "We don't want to get in trouble. So count us out for tonight. This isn't fun anymore."

Tim felt like a big rock had been lifted off his chest. No one was going along with Jon's plan. Annie's play was safe.

Then he had an idea. "People are getting tired of the Annoying Team, so let's get rid of it."

"Can you do that?" Judd asked.

"Sure," Tim said. "I started it. I can end it." He jumped out of his chair. "I'm nuking the Annoying Team! It's toast!"

"Burnt toast," Alex agreed happily.

Tim looked at the kids standing around his table. It reminded him of the day he'd

started the Annoying Team. He had felt so important then, and powerful. But right now, he felt even better.

"Okay, the Annoying Team is officially no more," Tim declared.

If Jon wanted to do something to Room 302's play, he could do it on his own. But Tim doubted that he would. Jon by himself wasn't that brave.

Tim sat down and leaned back in his lunchroom chair. Then something hit him. He knew he shouldn't think it. He knew he shouldn't be so glad about it. But he couldn't help it.

Wait until Jon found out the Annoying Team was finished. Nothing in the world would annoy him more.

About the Author

In Chicago, there once was a real-life Annoying Team. A nine-year-old boy told Ilene Cooper about a club he'd started at school to get back at kids who were teasing him.

"I asked Joshua if I could use the idea in a book and he agreed," Ilene says. "Like most people, Joshua thought a book gets published quickly. Here it is, five years later!"

Ilene Cooper is the author of *Buddy Love—Now on Video* and *Jack*, a biography of the young Jack Kennedy. She also wrote *Absolutely Lucy* and *Lucy on the Loose* for Golden Books.